Happy Mother's Day, Dear Dragon

Other Starfall Books
by Margaret Hillert

Not Too Little to Help
Penguin, Penguin
The No-Tail Cat
Three Little Plays

This book is part of the
"I'm Reading!" fluent reading sequence
featured on

www.**starfall**.com

This series is designed to encourage reading
fluency. It allows children to achieve mastery
and confidence by reading substantial books
(both fiction and non-fiction) which utilize a
limited vocabulary of sight words. "Step 1"
refers to the easiest group of books in this series.
It can be read after, or at the same time as,
Starfall's well-known Learn-to-Read phonics
series featuring Zac the Rat™ and other tales.

Text copyright © 2004 by Margaret Hillert.
Illustrations and graphics © 2004 Starfall Publications. All rights reserved.
Starfall is a registered trademark with the U.S. Patent and Trademark Office.
The content of this book is protected by the laws of copyright and trademark
in the U.S.A. and other countries. Printed in China.

ISBN: 1-59577-022-4

Starfall Publications
P.O. Box 359, Boulder, Colorado 80306

Happy Mother's Day, Dear Dragon

by Margaret Hillert

Illustrated by Craig Deeley

Starfall™
www.starfall.com

Come on.

Oh, come on now.

Get up. Get up.

I have to do something.

I have to make
something for Mother.
Can you help?

I want this —

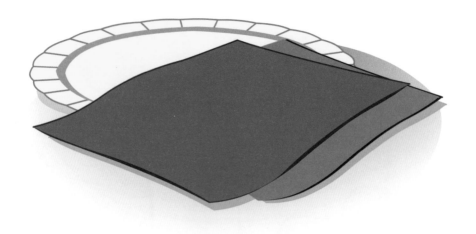

and this —

and this –

Now I will make
something pretty.
Red and yellow and blue.

Look at this.

Oh, this looks good.

Mother will like it.

Now come out here.

We have something to do here.

We will put this in here.
This is something good.

And we will make
something to eat.
This is good, too.

You can help.

Go out and get that.

Go, go, go.

Mother will want that.

You are a good help.
Come with me.
We will go to Mother.

Here we go.

Up, up, up.

Up to see Mother.

Get up, Mother. Get up.

We have something for you.

Get up and see what we have.

Oh, my. Oh, my.
What is this?
It is so pretty.
Did you make it?

And how good this looks.
I want to eat it.

Come here. Come here.

I want you to have something.

I love you.

Father, Father.
Do you have something
for Mother, too?

Yes, yes.

I do have something.

See what I have.

Red, yellow, and blue.

Come with me.

We will go down now.

Down, down, down.

Here you are with me.
And here I am with you.
Oh, what a happy Mother's Day,
Dear Dragon.

Vocabulary - 59 Words

a	happy	pretty
am	have	put
and	help	red
are	here	see
at	how	so
blue	I	something
can	in	that
come	is	this
day	it	to
dear	like	too
did	look(s)	up
do	love	want
down	make	we
dragon	me	what
eat	Mother('s)	will
Father	my	with
for	now	yellow
get	oh	yes
go	on	you
good	out	